llustrations by: Hà Tran

ISBN-13: 978-1536829662

FOR JACOB

Now go to sleep...

Chapitre 1: Dejeune
(Chapter One: Breakfast)

Mr. and Mrs. Valois awoke on a sunny Saturday morning to the familiar clink of the silver covered serving tray entering the room. Mr. Valois' hands searched for his eyeglasses on the night table, Mrs. Valois' feet for her furry lavender colored bunny slippers. As each found what they were looking for, the top of Francois head appeared at the foot of the bed.

As usual Francois was impeccably groomed, and as usual he wore a red bow-tie and carried a clean white towel over his arm. This morning he had awoken at first light to begin his duties as butler for Monsieur and Madame Valois. But Francois was not an ordinary butler. He was in fact, a third generation butler penguin. Francois' father and grandfather before him had both left the colony in Antarctica when they were Francois age and had ventured to far off lands to make their careers as distinguished butler penguins. And now, Francois had followed in their footsteps.

As the smell of fresh coffee met with Mr. Valois' nose he breathed in and sighed out contentedly. "Bonjour Francois."

"Bonjour Monsieur Valois"

"What is for breakfast this morning?" asked Mrs. Valois.

"Ah Madame, I have made something very special this morning", Francois was always trying to impress his employers with new recipes.

Mr. Valois sat up straighter trying to get a better look at the serving tray. Clearly Mr. Valois was very hungry.

Francois carefully positioned two blue coffee cups onto two matching blue saucers, and poured a cup of coffee for each of them. He then held up the silver tray to display his newest culinary creation.

"Voila!" said Francois as he whipped off the top of the serving tray and the strong smell of fish filled the Valois' bedroom.

Mr. Valois groaned audibly. Mrs. Valois' covered her nose with a blanket from the bed.

"Francois, what is that?!" asked Mr. Valois as he pointed to the tray, which was empty except for a large silver, nearly raw, fish.

"Ah sir, it is a mackerel, my personal favorite."

"Francois... mackerel is more of a penguin breakfast than a human breakfast" replied Mr. Valois trying to sound as grateful as he could for the meal Francois had prepared.

"Zut, Alors! I am sorry monsieur" said Francois, smacking his forehead with his free hand, his cheeks had turned nearly as red as his bow-tie with embarassment. He re-covered the dish and waddled quickly back to the kitchen to prepare a more human breakfast; though he was sure that humans didn't know what they were missing by turning down mackerel for any meal.

Chapitre 2: Gaston
(Chapter Two: Gaston)

The second breakfast Francois brought to the Valois bedroom had been much more to their tastes. Francois was back in the kitchen happily washing the dishes when he heard a small *tap*tap*tap* on the window above the kitchen sink. Wondering who would not have used the doorbell, Francois dried his hands on a towel and climbed down from the stepladder he used to get to the sink.

As he walked over to the side door, he could not see the silhouette of anyone through the drapes. "Perhaps it was just the milkman," he thought, as he strode up to the smaller penguin-sized side door inside the larger human one. As he undid the latch he heard a familiar gruff voice say "Enfin Francois, I thought you were going to leave me here all day."

Gaston was not a penguin-butler but a renown penguin-chef. He was legendary in the penguin service community for his fine pastries and desserts, and was employed at the neighbor's house just down the road from Francois

On this particular morning he had come to visit Francois in order to get a second opinion on his newest recipe.

Francois

Gaston

As the door swung inwards, a very round penguin, many years older, struggled to push his girth through the tiny Francois-sized door. With great effort and a loud popping noise he finally succeeded and now stood before Francois looking exhausted and more than a little embarrassed. "Bonjour Gaston!" beamed Francois, who was always happy to see his best friend.

"Bonjour Francois. It seems I may have been eating too many of my latest creation for breakfast" said the out-of-breathe Gaston as he revealed a small white cardboard box he was carrying under his arm.

"What is it Gaston?" asked Francois excitedly. He was always a willing test subject for Gaston's cooking. In fact, Francois thought most of Gaston's failures were quite delicious.

"Mon ami, Francois, I may have outdone myself this time" said Gaston confidently. He carefully unwrapped the package, revealing twelve small, perfectly round, perfectly identical pâtiserries. "And what do you call these" Francois asked, his mouth beginning to water.

"I call them "Choux à la crème du pingouin grande" beamed Gaston, as excited as Francois had ever seen him.

"The Creme puff of the grand penguin, wow Gaston, they must be magnificent!"

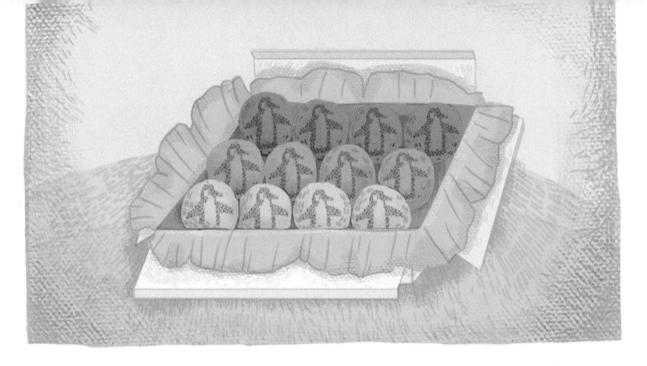

"Try one, and be honest about what you think" offered Gaston as he placed a single puff in front of Francois. As Francois examined the pastry, he noticed that the outside was a light brown color, but the pastry had been rolled in cocoa powder such that it resembled a penguin. Gaston smiled when he saw Francois notice this, he always took pride in the small details of his cooking.

Francois placed the puff in his mouth and after a moment "dèlicieux!" It was true Gaston had truly outdone himself this time.

"So you like them?" asked Gaston.

"Like them? C'est parfait! Perfect in every way" beamed Francois, who was now searching for the puff's eleven friends.

"I was considering entering them in the town baking competition next month."

"Absolument" interjected Francois, "you're a sure winner."

Gaston happily parted with the other creme puffs, and, after a brief chat about why humans can't fully appreciate mackerel, bid farewell to Francois when he remembered that he had to get back; there was another batch of puffs due to come out of the oven any minute.

Chapitre 3: La Livraison
(Chapter Three: The Delivery)

The Valois' would be spending the afternoon out with friends which left Francois with plenty of free time. Francois finished his kitchen duties and decided that, since it was a beautiful sunny day, he would spend some time outside in his garden.

The Valois had set aside a considerable portion of their yard for Francois to grow flowers and herbs, and Francois had transformed the area into a lush garden that resembled the French country estates he'd seen in his magazines. They were full of wonderfully scented herbs and colorful flowers of all different shapes and colors.

Francois put on his gardening gloves and his green galoshes and hung his towel and bow tie neatly on the coat rack just outside of his bedroom door. He went out of the penguin sized door in the kitchen and around the side of the house to the back yard. There he set out at once weeding and pruning where needed, all the while stopping by each plant to sample it's unique parfume. He was just about to finish cutting some fresh flowers for his room when he heard a large truck pull up to the Valois' house and stop.

"Très intéressant" thought Francois, Mr. Valois had not mentioned expecting any deliveries today. Francois brushed off his gardening gloves and clopped around to the front of the house in his galoshes where he saw Monsieur Dumont, their usual postman, struggling to lift a heavy box onto the porch.

"Bonjour Monsieur Dumont!" exclaimed Francois. "May I help you?"

"Ah, bonjour... bonjour Francois...no..I've got it...where should I put this?" panted Monsieur Dumont between heaves.

"What is it?" asked Francois.

"Je ne sais pas (I don't know) Francois, but its heavy and it's addressed to you" said Monsieur Dumont as he mopped his brow with a blue and white checked handkerchief.

"To me!" exclaimed Francois feeling his excitement grow. "Well we'd better put it in my cupboard."

"Ah bien" said Monsieur Dumont who was finally catching his breath.

Over the next 20 minutes, with a combination of pushing, pulling, begging, pleading, convincing, and maneuvering the two managed to move the large wooden box thru the foyer, thru the kitchen and finally into the adjoining cupboard through which lay Francois room.

Chapitre 4: La Garde-Manger
(Chapter Four: The Pantry)

The walk-in cupboard was small and cozy. And while Francois didn't require much space at all, he had nevertheless been thrilled to discover that it, in addition to his bedroom, would be his space when he first arrived at the Valois' house. It served as half-pantry for the kitchen, half-living room for Francois and he very much enjoyed relaxing in it during the evenings and on rainy days.

The room was well lit during the day by two large skylights that were positioned over the chaise, and at night by a small brass chandelier that hung neatly over a small round two-person table near the back of the room. Just past this table, further back in the cupboard, was a small wooden door that led to Francois' bedroom. This had previously been an extra room with a freezer for storing cold foods, but had been adapted to be the perfect sleeping quarters for a penguin butler, who felt most relaxed in the below freezing temperatures.

Toward the front of the room Francois had fashioned a comfortable chaise lounge out of several sacks of flour. Next to it stood a simple coffee table he had made out of wood that was several crates full of vegetables. When he first moved in, the Valois had offered to purchase any furnishings Francois desired, but Francois declined; He always preferred making things himself, he found he enjoyed them more that way.

Along two of the walls were long shelves, and while both still held food, Francois had made himself a little space on the lowest shelf for his small collection of books and several framed photos. Each shelf had a wooden ladder that slid on a brass track allowing Francois to reach everything.

Chapitre 5: La Surprise
(Chapter Five: The Surprise)

The room's newest addition, the mysterious wooden box that had just been delivered, now stood next to the chaise lounge and coffee table. After catching their breath Monsieur Dumont had accepted a cold drink and the two parted company feeling quite accomplished.

The box was slightly taller than Francois and its wood paneled sides stood covered in the postage and customs stamps of a half dozen countries. Francois recognized the stamps from France, New Zealand, and Belgium. But it seemed this trunk had traveled quite a bit further...there were also stamps from Peru, China, Morocco, and Vietnam! And buried under these other markings Francois found a stamp he was very familiar with, Antarctica! With a pang of nostalgia, Francois realized this was a trunk from his parents. He climbed on top of his chaise lounge and managed to pry off the top of the crate using a garden spade as a crowbar.

As he excitedly slid the lid off to the side, he saw a short postcard type note on the top of the packing materials. It read:

Dear Francois,

Congratulations! Your father and I are so proud of you for graduating from St. Buttlesmore Academy. The penguin butler academy is as prestigious as it is challenging. Your father will never admit it, but he was thrilled when you chose to follow in his and grandpa's footsteps to become a penguin-butler.

Now that you're a penguin-butler, do you have any idea where you want to go for work? Well, wherever you go, I thought you'd like a few things from your room to make you feel more at home. We know you're very busy! Write when you get a chance.

Adore (Love),
Maman (mum)

Francois was immediately overcome by feelings of nostalgia for home and his parents. He walked to the shelf in the pantry that held all of his pictures and pulled down the picture of him with his mom and dad from just before he went off to St. Buttlesmore. They were standing just in front of their home back in Antarctica, Francois between his two beaming parents holding his St. Buttlesmore acceptance letter high.

Francois returned to the box in the middle of the room and began investigating its other contents. Every layer contained another wonderful surprise.

Premier (First),

On top, Francois' found nine new white towels. Each had a stately F embroidered in red thread near the top. Francois mother would make these for him by the dozen when he was still at St. Buttlesmore. Below that he found a large-by-penguin-standards blanket that his mother had knitted for him. The blanket was dark blue with dozens of white snowflakes, and very soft.

Deuxième (Second),

Underneath, cushioned by the towels and blanket, were several pictures of the family; including one of his entire extended family holding a large banner reading "Congratulations Francois!" A St. Buttlesmore pennant was tucked neatly next to it.

Troisième (Third):

Beneath the pictures and pennant was a layer of bubble-wrap. As Francois peeled back this layer he, to his great delight, found dozens of tins full of his favorite smoked mackerel snacks. He had been unable to locate them at any of the grocery stores near the Valois' residence. Francois now realized what had made the crate so heavy! His mother knew how much he loved them and now he had smoked mackerel snacks for months.

Francois ate two entire tins of mackerel snacks straightaway and spent the remainder of the afternoon situating his new things. Then he sat down to write his parents thanking them and letting them know the trunk had finally arrived.

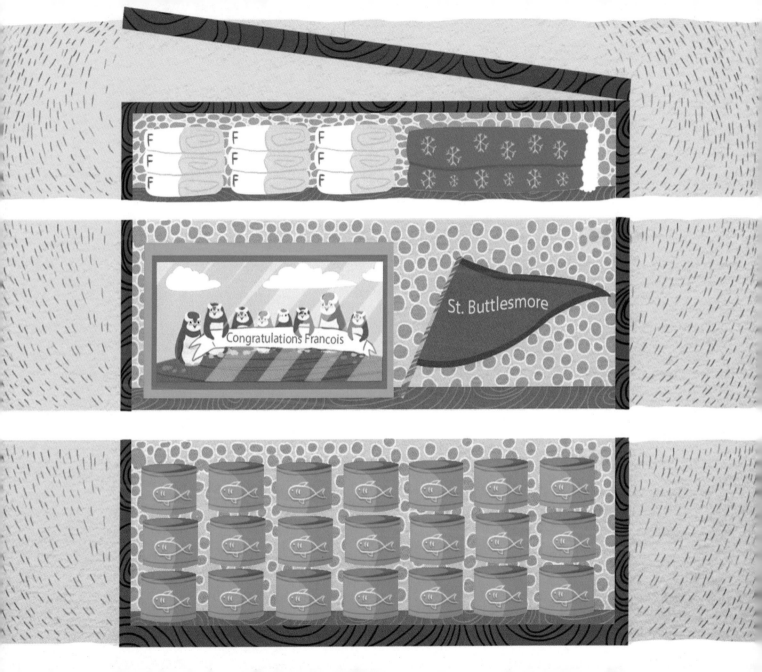

Chapitre 6: Le Pingouin dans le Congélateur
(Chapter Six: The Penguin in the freezer)

It was getting late and Francois was out at the mailbox depositing his letter to his parents just as Monsieur and Madame Valois returned.

"Bonjour Francois" said a very tired Madame Valois.

"Welcome Back Madame!" replied Francois. "Would you like me to prepare something for dinner?"

"Merci Francois, but that won't be necessary, we are just returning from dinner." replied an equally tired Monsieur Valois as they headed inside. "How was your day?"

"Ah Monsieur, tres bien!" exclaimed Francois.

They sat around the table as Francois told them all about Gaston's cream puffs, his garden, and then about the delivery and it's contents. He then finished by telling them about the letter from his parents.

"Well, it sounds like your day was very exciting Francois" said Madame Valois as Francois wrapped up his story.

"Oui Madame very exciting indeed" said Francois through a yawn, now realizing how tired all of this had made him. The Valois, who were very tired themselves stood from the table.

"Will you need anything else tonight" asked Francois as the Valois turned to head upstairs.

"Non, Francois. Merci Beaucoup. Bonsoir."

"Bonsoir Monsieur, Madame."

Francois made his way into the pantry, where he helped himself to one final mackerel snack before bed. He hung his red bowtie and white towel neatly on the coat rack and put on his pajamas; then made his way through the door to his bedroom.

Francois' bedroom was lit by a small chandelier hanging overhead, and the floor was almost completely filled with the large white lay down "Frost King" freezer. The walls were covered in pictures set in simple frames; some Francois had taken, some he had painted, and some that were gifts from friends. On the front of the freezer was a small Francois-sized door with a small set of steps.

Francois then got ready for bed. He brushed his teeth, and washed his hands and face before slipping into a pair of pajamas. After a brief look at all of his pictures, Francois turned out the overhead light and ascended the steps.

He climbed thru the door into the freezer and, as the cold reached him, he suddenly felt very comfortable. Though Francois had adapted to the warmer climate where the Valois lived, he always felt the most comfortable in the sharp cold.

Inside of the freezer was lit from a small appliance light that Francois often used to read with. But tonight he was much too sleepy! His bed, several large bags of frozen "Donne-moi" brand French peas, sat neatly made at the back of the freezer. Francois walked over to it, climbed in, and tucked the new snowflake blanket from his mom up to his chin. With one final yawn, he reached up and turned out the light. Francois fell asleep thinking about how wonderful his day had been.

Made in the USA
Columbia, SC
19 August 2021